The Secret in the Water

Antoinette Sidberry Richardson

PAGE PUBLISHING
Conneaut Lake, PA

First originally published by Page Publishing 2023

ISBN 979-8-88793-812-7 (pbk)
ISBN 979-8-88793-813-4 (digital)

Printed in the United States of America

This is a story about a sweet old woman named Gracy who lived alone in a small but adorable cottage deep in the forest. You see, Gracy lived alone because she had never married and never had any children. But even though she was alone, Gracy loved everything about where she lived. It was so exciting to wake up early every morning just to see what had grown in her garden and imagine what her life could be like.

Her home was simple and clean with pretty flowers and trees all around it, and her cottage was whitewashed with a little green trim. There was also a town with a market where you could trade and buy things not too far from where she lived. It was always fun to go there.

One morning, after a long peaceful night, Gracy pulled her aching body up out of bed and gave it a big stretch, then moved over to a big white mirror trimmed in pink that was anchored to the wall. It was a gift from her mother when she was a child. Squinting her eyes to look at her white hair and the deep wrinkles on her face, she started to think to herself, *Where has the time gone? I am an old woman now.*

This day Gracy was feeling her best. She danced to her closet just to pick out one of the three dresses she made, did a little spin, and laid it across the soft chair sitting by the door in her room. Looking at her choice, she said, "Today I will wear my blue flowed dress with the green trim and my favorite brown shoes." After grooming herself from top to bottom and getting dressed for the day, she would always walk through her house, open every window just to hear the birds sing, smell the flowers, and see how the wind blew through the trees.

Taking a walk through the forest to gather fruit and berries was a must. Gracy loved eating them for her breakfast. She was always wondering what it would have been like to have a husband and children. She thought, *If only I could turn back the time and become my young and beautiful self again. Silly me, that could never happen, but never say never with a smile.*

One morning, when Gracy was out working in her garden, she decided to take a long walk. "I think I will go to town today," Gracy said to herself. So she grabbed her basket just in case she saw something she would like to bring home. Even if she didn't see anything at the market, sometimes things just fall from the trees, like her favorite fruits and berries.

On her way down the path, she decided to take a different way. While thinking over her life, she imagined she was holding the hand of a child, spinning and turning and laughing to herself, and saying there was nothing wrong with being hopeful even though she was old. Being a mom and a wife was never far from her mind.

All of a sudden, she realized she had walked farther than she had ever walked before. When Gracy started to turn back, she noticed something strange. "What is that?" she said to herself. "Oh my lord!" It was the biggest and the most beautiful house she had ever seen. It was made with gray stones, one a little darker than the other. The windows were trimmed in gold with a light shining from within the house, which made some pretty patterns on the ground. There were bright flowers and colorful trees all around it and an unusually shaped well for drinking nice cool water, and it had some amazing rocks placed all around the bottom in place, just right. Gracy could tell there was a cozy fire in the fireplace because she could see smoke coming from the chimney disappearing into the sky with the wind.

Who could live in such a place? Gracy thought. *Maybe I'll go and introduce myself mainly so I can get a closer look.*

As she started to walk up to the door, she could smell something wonderful cooking. This made her stomach growl. *That is not fruits and berries*, she thought.

Right when she was getting ready to knock on the big brown door, she heard a loud noise. Gracy changed her mind and walked away very quickly as if she was in a rush.

That night, while Gracy was eating dinner, she could not stop thinking about the strange but beautiful big house. It was so amazing, she just had to see it again. After cleaning her kitchen and preparing herself for bed, Gracy struggled to fall asleep, tossing and turning most of the night. She finally dozed off with her head filled with all kinds of amazing things about the house, and this gave Gracy a wonderful dream.

The next morning, she got up early as always, but she did not stop to open the windows, listen to the birds sing, smell the flowers, or watch the way the wind blew through the trees. She just grabbed her shawl and walked very fast to the beautiful house. When she got there, she saw a funny-looking old man who looked like he was working on something exciting in the yard. Gracy stood and just watched him for a moment. Then the old man started to sing, "What will I do with my fountain of youth, my fountain, my fountain of youth?"

Gracy thought, *He is singing a song about a fountain, not just any fountain. Oh no! He is singing about a fountain of youth!*

Gracy listened very closely to the song, and the old man began to sing the song again. "What will I do with my fountain, my fountain of youth?"

"I wonder if it's true," Gracy said to herself. "I could turn back time get married and have children. "Maybe if I could just ask him. Surely a person who lives in such a house would be very nice. After all, we are neighbors." In her very sweet voice, Gracy called out to him, "Hello!"

The old man turned and looked at Gracy from her head to her feet and said, "Who are you?"

"I'm Gracy," she said. "I live in the small cottage down the path."

Just as she was speaking, the old man butted in with a nasty-sounding voice, "Okay! Okay! Old lady, what do you want?"

"Well, I heard you singing that song."

"What song?" said the old man.

With confusion on her face, she replied, "The song about the fountain."

"What fountain?" said the old man.

Looking even more confused, she said, "The fountain of youth." Then she smiled. "And I was hoping you would tell me about it."

"No!" the old man replied in his nasty voice. "I will not tell you anything! Now gets away from my house." The old man started walking away, but then he stopped.

Gracy was a little afraid of the old man, but she wanted to know if the song was true. So she asked him again, "Oh, please, mister, please tell me if the song is true." Gracy started to explain. "You see, I have never been married, and I don't have any children."

As Gracy was telling her story the old man butted in, "Of course. I don't care if you are alone. I will never tell you anything."

With tears in her eyes and a sad look on her face, Gracy said once again, "Oh, please."

The old man folded his arms, turned his head, looked at Gracy with a frown on his mean-looking face, showing his ugly yellow teeth, and said, "For the third time, *no!*"

Then he reached down and picked up a stick and swung it at Gracy. She screamed out in disbelief and fear in her voice, "Please, don't hit me! I will go!" Then she turned and walked away.

The old man screamed at her in his nastiest voice while waving the stick, "And stay away from my house!"

On the way home, Gracy started to cry. She had never met anyone like that before. She thought, *He is mean and nasty, and I don't understand why he will not help me.* The more she thought about how the old man treated her, the sadder she got. Gracy just could not believe or understand how someone could be so mean and selfish.

After walking back down the path, she finally arrived at her small cottage. As she turned the doorknob and stepped through and over the door frame, her foot scraped the bottom of her shoe. Gracy kicked off her shoes and walked through the house, straight to her room, to get ready for bed. With tears still streaming down her face, Gracy dropped her arms to her side in defeat. After wiping the tears from her face, she went to look at herself in her big round white mirror trimmed in pink. Her eyes were red along with her nose. Gracy still could not believe what had happened. She leaned over. Putting both hands over her face, she started to cry all over again. Moving her hands past her forehead, Gracy pulled her fingers through her very soft and white hair as if they were a comb. She moved her hands over to the side of her face and pulled her skin back to smooth out the wrinkles as if they were never there. "If only I can turn back time," she whispered to herself. She slowly let go, and everything started to relax, and the reality of her long life and wrinkles formed back into place as if she had never smoothed them out in the first place. But this did not make her sad. Gracy thought of the fountain, the song, and the old man, knowing she had a chance to change her look to put a big smile back on her face.

As Gracy continued to stare at herself in the mirror, something came over her that night. With her head tilted to the side and a gleam in her eye, it all changed her into a sneaky person. "I must find out!" she said. "If he will not tell me, I'll just have to find out another way."

She continued her nightly routine and settled into bed. While lying there, Gracy made a list of things she wanted to do when she became young again, then she came up with a brilliant idea. "If he will not tell me, then I'll just have to find out another way."

So the next morning, Gracy jumped up with so much excitement. She ate breakfast, cleaned her house from top to bottom, and wrote down on paper a list of things she wanted to do after she became young again. Gracy was so determined to have the best life she could imagine. After she completed everything, she decided to return to the old man's house. Her plan was to watch and follow him every day, and maybe, just maybe, he would lead her to his fountain of youth, if there is one. She put her list on the table so she could look at it every day.

Before Gracy left her cottage, she remembered that there was a well at the end of the yard in front of the old man's house. *Could that be the fountain of youth?* she thought. *Is that what he was singing about?* So she decided to carry a small bottle for the water. She put everything she thought was needed in her basket, then she said to herself, "Okay, Gracy, one last check. I have my favorite shawl, some fruit, berries, a stick, and a bottle to fill with water. All there." She was ready for anything.

It was time to walk down the path to the old man's house. This time the walk did not seem as long. When she got there, to her surprise, the old man was in the yard, getting water from the well. Gracy slowly backed away and sat where he could not see her. Every day there was one reason after the next that she could not get to the well: the old man was always doing something in the yard. But Gracy did not give up. Day after day, she would just sit and watch. As the week went on, Gracy's back and legs started to hurt; all the walking, sitting, and bending were starting to hurt her body. But once again Gracy went down the path to the old man's house, watching and snooping.

This day that nasty old man came out of his beautiful house, carrying his water bucket. He walked past the well and hummed to himself. Gracy thought this might be her chance. "The old man always gets the water and returns to the house, so as soon as he walks away, I'll run over and get some water very fast. But very fast to an old woman wasn't fast at all. I think I will just wait," she said to herself as she took a big breath and dropped back down.

But wait, this day was different. The old man walked around to the back of his house. *Where is he going?* Gracy thought. She couldn't help herself; she had to follow him. Gracy saw that the bucket he was carrying was different from the one he usually carried to the well. This one was blue. The other one was bright red.

After all this time, she had never been around the back of the house before. There was a woodpile for the fireplace with an ax for chopping it and a line for hanging out laundry. Even though Gracy was curious about the things in the backyard, she needed to keep up with the old man. Following him was a challenge. Gracy's feet were starting to hurt worse, so she had to slow down a bit. Then the bit became a lot. Falling more and more behind, she was still just able to see where he was going from afar.

In the distance, Gracy kept her eyes on him so she could continue to follow the funny old man. Trying to catch up, she stumbled a few times, but she kept her eye on the old man and the bucket. One time she even had to stop and lean, which helped Gracy to stay back so he would not see her. She was determined to see where he was going as he took an extra skip and hop right back into his walk, swinging his bucket.

Then the old man started to sing his song. "What will I do with my fountain, my fountain of youth?" He would sing it over and over. Now Gracy knew for sure he was on his way to the fountain. This gave her a little more energy and a pep in her step, but it seemed like they had been walking forever.

"This is a long dark path," Gracy said to herself. "I have never been this far from my cottage before."

Finally, after walking down the long dark path, the old man stopped at this unkept little broken-down house. This part of the forest was dark and scary, and Gracy had no idea where she was! The old man went into the strange house and stayed for a while, so she sat down as close as she could to the house without the old man seeing her. Gracy put her shawl over her head and fell asleep. She was so tired, and her back and feet hurt.

While Gracy was asleep, she dreamed of all the things she would do once she was young again. Oh, how much fun she's going to have. In the middle of her sweet dream, Gracy was awakened out of her sleep by a nasty loud voice saying, "What are you doing here?" She jumped with fear and started to sweat. Her mouth was dry, and at first not a word would come! When her eyes focused, she saw the old man standing over her.

"Have you been following me?" he yelled.

Gracy swallowed hard and deep with her head still down. She answered, "Yes! But I only wanted to find out if it's true about the fountain of youth."

The old man replied, "Well, I guess you will never leave me alone unless I show you! So come on!" Then he started to walk deeper into the forest. The deeper they went, the darker it got. Then finally they came to a bright beautiful pond. It was such an amazing place with colorful flowers all around, a trail of rocks with water running through the gap and separating at just the right point to create tiny drops of water that presented a rainbow that landed all so well to show the beauty of it. Surrounding the pond were some of the same rocks placed around the well at the old man's house.

This must be where he got them from, Gracy thought. She could not believe her eyes. Everything was so beautiful. She had joy in her heart that she was finally there. It was her dream. Gracy was also leaping with joy on the inside as she was taking it all in, thinking about all her hopes and dreams that would finally come true.

The old man yelled at her, "Well, what are you waiting for? Drink!"

After Gracy got herself together from being yelled at, she slowly bent down her aching body from being old and, of course, the long walk. She put her wrinkled hands together, dipped them into the water, and raised them slowly to her mouth. With her eyes closed, she began to drink.

Splash! The old man pushed her in. With her heart pounding and struggling to pull herself out, Gracy noticed she was getting smaller. Grabbing onto anything to save herself, she realized she could stand and walk. She moved closer to the edge so she could stretch out her hands, hoping to get a grip on a branch, rock, or something, while the old man just stood by with a smile on his face and watched. Finally she got a grip on a stone and pulled herself safely back onto dry land.

Standing there with water dripping from her dress and shivering because she was now wet and cold, her body began to feel different. She could see better, and her feet and back didn't hurt anymore. Looking down at her hands, she saw the wrinkles were gone. Her shoes were wet and too big, and her dress was just hanging on her like a rag doll. After Gracy got herself together, she walked around to the other side of the pond to get a good look at herself. Thinking the old man might push her in again, she stayed away and kept an eye on him. When she saw her reflection in the water, Gracy gasped. She was a child. Her hair was now blonde instead of gray, and her face was smooth with no wrinkles. She loved it, but she was too young. Once again she started to cry.

The old man said, "What are you crying for? Isn't this what you wanted? Now you got it!"

In her moment of sadness, Gracy said yes, but I only wanted to be a little younger, I did not want to be a child, look at me, "I'm a little girl!"

The old man said, "Of course you didn't want to be a child, but I wanted to teach you a lesson. You've been snooping around my house for a week. You thought I didn't know? I saw you every time. I was waiting for my chance to lead you here. You thought you were so smart. Now the tricks are on you."

Gracy yelled out, "Now I might not ever get married and have children! I need to go home to my cottage and think about what I need to do."

The old man replied, "Well, you can just stop thinking about that. You being a child gives me my complete set, three and three."

Gracy had no idea what he was talking about.

"From now on you will live with me. Yes, I finally have my complete set."

Gracy did not understand why he wanted her to live with him or what he was talking about, but she was very afraid. Then the old man dipped his bucket deep in the water and grabbed Gracy by her small hand, pulling her very fast through the forest. When Gracy and the other man reached his house, he said to her, "Now, my Ms. Nosey, it's time for you to get to work." Then he opened the big wooden door to the beautiful big gray house and pushed her in. Gracy stumbled to the floor, scraping her hand from trying to catch herself. She stayed in that position for just a moment. Gracy pushed herself up from the floor, leaving a small bloodstain from the cut on her hand when she fell.

Then the old man looked around and said, "You over there, Elaine, you will show her what to do, and make sure she does everything right. Now get to work." He pushed Gracy again but toward Elaine this time. As Gracy was being pushed, Elaine was already walking over to her. When they were face-to-face She started demonstrating to Gracy what her job would be: cleaning the floors in the dining room and the kitchen after breakfast and dinner were served. The second oldest girl, Emily, had to make sure all the plates, cups, forks, spoons, pots, and pans were washed and put away. Tony would go hunting with the old man to bring back food. Lee would clean whatever Tony and the old man brought back from their hunt. For some reason, the old man trusted Elaine to tell the others what to do, to prepare his meals, and to be his eyes and ears when he wasn't there. Mike, the youngest of them all, would take out the trash after all the work was done.

Now that Gracy knew what was expected of her, she stopped to look around for just a moment.

Everyone was busy at work. She was trying to figure out why no one was talking, so once the old man was out of the house, she decided to ask, "Why isn't anyone talking?"

Every child looked at her with fear in their eyes and did not say a word. Finally Elaine pulled her by the arm away from the other children and explained all the rules of the house. They were not allowed to talk to one another. She didn't know why; they just weren't.

Gracy asked, "What will happen if we do?"

Elaine said, "If the old man heard us talking or if he even found out that we were talking, he would be very upset, and all of us would be in serious trouble. We are only allowed to work eat and drink water from the blue bucket, that's all."

Gracy was in so much disbelief that she let her greed get her into this situation, and she had no idea how to change it back. The thought of not being able to talk, sing, dance, or do anything made her sick to the stomach. *What have I done? If only I have been satisfied with my life the way it was.* Sadness was all over Gracy's little face. She went over to the big brown door, turned the knob, and tried to pull it open. It was locked from the outside. Gracy dropped to the floor, looked to the left side of her, and saw the bloodstain from her hand when she fell earlier. She wet her finger with her spit and rubbed it until it was gone.

All the children came around because they knew how she was feeling. Tony reached out his hand to help Gracy up, and Elaine wiped away her tears.

Then Gracy grab her dress and tied a knot at the bottom to make it shorter now that it was too long. She found something soft to put in her shoes because they were big as well. Gracy did everything she was told to do. She worked hard and cried every day, wishing she was actually in a dream so she could wake up to being old Gracy again. Now that Gracy was living with the old man and the other children, she would get up early every morning as always. But she could not open the windows, smell the flowers, hear the birds, see how the wind was blowing through the trees, or take a look in the mirror her mother had given her when she was a child. No walks to gather fruits and berries or work in her garden. She could not go to the market in town. Her life was now all about what someone else wanted her to do. She could not even remember where she left her favorite shawl. *I know I had it when the old man pushed me into the pond. I guess I will never see it again*, Gracy thought.

Gracy continued to do her chores and had time to help the other children with theirs, at the same time making up songs and happy thoughts in her head. Day after day it was all the same. As the days turned into weeks and the weeks turned into months, Gracy never complained. She worked until her hands were bruised. Gracy would often find herself looking at the other children and wondering, *Where did the other children come from? Did he push them in the water as well, or are they just children?*

Elaine was pretty with long red hair that stuck to the side of her face from working hard with sweat streaming down across her forehead. She had a few dresses to change one in per tickler that reminded Gracy of the curtains in her cottage. Everything fit her.

Emily was short and cute as a button. She always seemed to have a smile on her face with her little legs all scared up from bumping them on the ladder as she climbed up to put away the dishes. With her blonde hair, blue eyes, and freckles, she looked to be about ten.

Mike, the youngest, looked just like Emily but only a boy and a little chubby. He struggled with the garbage every night, but he got the job done. Gracy would often see him in a corner getting an extra bite to eat and usually with tears in his eyes.

Lee cleaned the kill of the day with his dark hair and big brown eyes and always tripped over his feet. Gracy was not sure, but she thought he was about twelve maybe.

Tony was tall and handsome with olive skin, green eyes, and jet-black hair. He's the oldest of the boys and the biggest, which gave him the most responsibility outside the house. For some reason, he would always look at this gold pocket watch when the old man was not around.

Above all that, each child had a special garment that was handpicked by the old man. Nothing fit anyone properly except for Elaine—her dress fit her perfectly. Emily was kind of pretty, but she was given a pair of the ugliest shoes she had ever seen.

Looking down at her dress, Gracy wondered if she would get a special garment as well and hoped it would be a pretty dress like Elaine's.

One day the old man said to Gracy, "I need you to go down the dark path to get the water from the pond." She thought, *Why do we need water from the pond when there is a well right there?* But she dared not to ask; she just did as she was told. So Gracy walked past the old man to the corner behind him and picked up a blue bucket that was sitting in front of his hunting gear. Carrying it in her right hand, she swiftly walked out the door. Once she was out of the house, she stood for a second, took a deep breath of fresh air, and started down the long dark path, taking a glance in the well at the end of the yard as she walked by. She still didn't understand why they needed the well water.

Down the path she went, passing the other strange house to get to the pond. She thought back to the night she followed the old man and he stopped at this same house. Gracy just looked at it as she walked very fast to the pond. When she got there, she bent over, dropped the bucket into the water, and filled it as much as she could, holding it with both hands. Then she started her walk back, trying hard not to spill a drop. Gracy was moving as fast as she could back down the long dark path. When she was almost back, her hands started to burn from the handle of the bucket. Adjusting her hands for more comfort made it a little easier.

When she returned to the house, the old man took one look at the bucket of water and said, "From now on, getting the water from the pond will be your responsibility."

Gracy was so happy about getting to take walks, but she could not show how excited she was. It made no difference that she was afraid of the long dark path. She just loved being able to leave the house. It gave her time to think, smell the flowers, listen to the birds sing, and see how the wind blew through the trees. She could even sing and dance on the way. It would be a new adventure every time. *This is going to be great!* Gracy thought.

That night, at dinner, Gracy did not even care that she was drinking the water from the pond. She was just so excited that in two days, she would be able to go back for her long walk. *Water or no water, I get to walk.* She didn't even realize she was smiling to herself.

The old man hit his hand on the table. "What are you smiling about, girl?"

Gracy and the other children jumped. Lee knocked over his water, and the old man gave him a mean look. Elaine ran to get a cloth to wipe up the water. Gracy just sat there in silence.

"I asked you a question." The old man leaned toward Gracy. "What are you smiling about?"

"I didn't know I was smiling. I was trying to get something out of my tooth."

"You listen to me. You don't smile, talk, or try to run away! You hear me, girl?" the old man said.

"Yes!" said Gracy with tears in her eyes.

Elaine looked at her with much compassion. Tony, Mike, and Emily looked at her with much compassion. They, along with Lee, just dropped their heads and continued eating. Gracy didn't want to eat another bite, but she knew she had to. So she sat there and stuffed it all down.

The next day Gracy got up and worked harder than she had on all the other days she'd been at the old man's house. She found herself happier than usual. It was a nice but unusually hot day. Gracy grabbed the blue bucket and started her walk down the path. By the time she approached the pond, she was very tired and exhausted from the heat. She got down on her knees and bent over to wash her face when she saw her reflection in the water. She would often do this because she had no mirror in the old man's house. *I'm beautiful, but I am a child,* she thought as she sat down to continue to look at herself. She saw a reflection of someone standing behind her. Gracy jumped and looked over her shoulder. It was gone. Then she jumped up hurried to dip the bucket in the water and ran down the dark path. She ran so fast that by the time she got to the house, half of the water had spilled out. "Oh no, the old man will be very mad with me," said Gracy. So she stopped to add some of the water from the well at the end of the yard. She was sure to fill the bucket almost to the top and carried it into the house with both hands, trying not to spill any on the floor and not make any mess for her or someone to clean up.

Gracy walked across the room to set the bucket down. Out of the corner of her eye, she saw the old man looking at her. She was worried he had seen her fill the bucket with the well water.

"It took you a long time to get that water, girl. What have you been doing?" the old man said in his nasty voice.

"I just sat down for a moment because I was a little hot and tired," said Gracy in a very shaky voice.

The old man just looked at her for a moment, and Gracy did not move an inch. "Ah, just get to work," said the old man.

As Gracy started to work, she could not stop thinking about the reflection she saw watching over her at the pond. Now that she was over her fear of walking down the dark path and passing the other strange house, she had something else to worry about. This made her a little more afraid to go back, but she knew she would have to.

After Gracy and the other children completed all their work, they all sat down at the table to eat.

The oldest girl, Elaine, would always serve the old man first; and what was left she gave to Gracy and the other children. Now it was time for the water. When Elaine was giving the old man his glass of water, Gracy watched her and the old man. It was terrifying to think he would taste the difference in the water. But then she noticed that his glass of water was from a different bucket; it was silver. Elaine did not get his water from the one she brought in from the pond; only she and the other children were being served from it. She had never noticed it before, but what was he drinking? Now she just figured out why he was so old. He's not drinking from the fountain of youth. That's it! The secret was in the water. *If we can only drink the mixed water, we should grow old again!* She was so beside herself; trying not to smile or dance was hard.

At the end of the week, it was once again time for Gracy to go down the dark path to get the water. She could not stop thinking about what she saw the last time she was there. This time Gracy ran down the path as fast as she could, dipped the bucket in the water, then walked very fast back to the house. When she returned, she saw the youngest girl, Emily, cleaning in front of the house, which was unusual. *Why isn't she in the kitchen?* Gracy thought.

Then Emily whispered to Gracy, "I've been waiting for you."

"Why?" said Gracy.

"I'm starting to feel different. Are you?" said Emily.

At first she could not believe she was actually talking to her, but in spite of that, she answered "Yes, I do" with a big smile on her face.

"I wonder why," said Emily.

Gracy thought it must be because she had mixed the fountain water with the well water. She looked at Emily and noticed she was a little taller. *It is changing us already. We are growing and getting older*, Gracy thought. But she dared not say anything. *I need to find a way to get us all out of here before the old man notices.*

That night, Gracy took a big chance and told all the other children what had happened to the water. "Make sure you continue to drink it like always." As the weeks went by, Gracy noticed that all the children were starting to get even bigger except for one the boy named Tony. She could not understand why the other children were growing but not him. That made Gracy pray every night that the old man would not notice that she and the other children were getting older. Gracy decided to talk to Tony when she got a chance. She would ask him, and when she got the chance, she did. "Are you still drinking nothing but the pond water?" said Gracy.

Tony said yes.

She asked him why.

"Because I'm afraid not to!"

Gracy told him, "You have to stop so we all can look the same and we all can have a chance to get out of here."

"I don't think I want to go. I'm afraid," said Tony.

"Don't be. We all will be with you."

To Tony's agreement, he decided to drink the mixed water. Now the children were afraid, but just thinking that they might be able to get out of the old man's house gave them the courage to talk to one another more. They even made a joke that the old man might push them into the pond or make them drink more than they need.

Now Gracy had been dreading going down the dark path to get the water only because she didn't want to run into whatever that was she saw at the time she was there, but for the sake of her and her new family getting away from the old man, she had to be brave. So once again Gracy grabbed the bucket and started down the long dark path, hoping not to see anything. As she was walking, an image appeared in front of her. She turned to run, and there it was again. Gracy covered her face with her hands, hoping it would go away. She peeked through her fingers, and it was gone. She started walking in the other direction while looking all around her, then Gracy stopped. She saw someone standing at the end of the path. It was Tony. "What are you doing here?" Gracy said.

With a concerned look on his face, he replied, "I decided to come and get my own water."

"Why?" said Gracy.

"Because I'm so afraid the old man would notice that I'm getting older!" He threw his hands up in the air and dropped them and his head at the same time. "I have to go hunting with him tomorrow."

"But we have been very careful," said Gracy.

"I know," said Tony. "But I'm growing faster than everyone else."

"Tony, you have always been bigger than us all. That's why I know you can help everyone. Okay, I'll tell you what, if it makes you feel better, start drinking only the pond water again, and we will drink the pond water mixed with the well water," said Gracy. Then she hugged him so as to say, "It's going to be okay. Now we must run."

They both noticed that they had been gone a long time. So as fast as they could, the two of them ran down the dark path. This time Tony was caring the bucket. Meanwhile, Gracy was still looking around for the strange object that would be at the pond whenever she was there.

Before they reached the house, Gracy took the bucket of water, added the well water, and went into the house. Tony took a different route to make sure they were not seen together. After their talk at the fountain, now he and Gracy had a plan, and they were working together. From then on, every night, she made sure the children would drink only the mixed glass of water. Unknown to Gracy, Tony had stopped drinking the fountain water. He decided on his just in case the other children started to grow faster.

One day, when everyone was working in the house, Gracy noticed that Mike was just as tall as Tony. She motioned for him to come to her. "Are you still drinking just the pond water?"

"No," said Tony. "I've been drinking a little of both."

"Mike is getting big. He is just about your size! We have to find a way to get out of here," she said with worry on her face.

"Okay, next time the old man goes out alone, we will run," said Tony.

"But wait, the door is always locked when he goes out," said Gracy.

Tony said, "Do you remember when you saw me at the pond? I know another way out."

"Okay, we will go your way." With fear and excitement, Gracy's eyes lit up, and with a big smile she said, "Yes! Once we are out, I can lead everyone to my cottage through the forest. I don't think the old man knows where it is. Besides, we have to take that chance."

"That's right," Mike said.

Then Gracy made sure everyone knew the plan. They were all excited but continued to work as usual. Most days the old man would take one or two of the boys with him. Gracy wondered why they would never talk about where the old man would take them. When they brought back a dead animal, she knew they went hunting; when they brought food, they went to the market. On other days they had nothing at all. There were times when the old man would be very mean to each child, some days more than others, with a lot of pushing and yelling.

Finally the day was here. The old man was gone, and he left everyone. Tony said, "*Okay*, Gracy, let's get Elaine, Mike, Lee, and Emily out of here." So Tony yelled out, "Grab only the things you love the most, and let's go!"

Sweet Emily grabbed her favorite doll. It had a dress that was her favorite color, pink. This doll was also her best friend. At night she could tell it her deepest secrets and dreams. Emily loved her doll.

Mike said, "I have the jacket my mom made for me." His jacket was blue with lots of pockets for hiding things; he had a lot hidden in them. That statement made Gracy's will to get them out even faster.

Lee loved his shoes. He didn't say why, but they were just big.

Tony said he loved everyone in the room.

Just when Gracy was getting ready to speak, Elaine gave Gracy her shawl that she thought she would never see again. Her eyes were filled with tears. "Where did you find this, and how did you know it was mine?"

Elaine said, "I was one of the first of the children to be kidnaped by the old man. He always kept something from each child put away in his room."

Gracy looked at Elaine, pushed her red hair back from her face, and hugged her with such love as a mother would to her daughter. Gracy whispered in her ear, "I love you."

"Okay, come on everyone. Let's get out of here. The old man will be back soon." Tony said. They all followed him to the secret door. He led them to the back of the house and pushed the wall. It opened to the outside right next to the woodpile. The wind was really blowing hard. It made it hard to keep the door open. While Tony was holding the door open for everyone to come out, Gracy stood on the inside to make sure they all came through. One by one they ran out the door, each one waiting for the rest to come out.

Elaine was last before Gracy. She stopped at the door and yelled out, "I change my mind. I don't want to go!"

Gracy looked at her with a lack of understanding on her face because she didn't really hear her, "What did you say?" said Gracy.

Elaine looked at Gracy and said, "I change my mind. I don't want to go."

Gracy asked why.

"I just don't want to go!"

All the while Tony was calling out, "Come on, we have to go!"

"I don't want to leave you, Emily," said Gracy.

"Please go," said Elaine. "I will be all right."

"No," said Gracy with tears in her eyes. "I don't want to leave you!"

Tony ran over to see what was going on, and Gracy said, "Elaine doesn't want to come with us. She's afraid."

"Just go," said Elaine. "I will be okay. I love you all, but you have to go!"

Not wanting to leave her, Gracy said, "I love you too. Then Tony, Gracy, Emily, Mike, and Lee started running toward Gracy's cottage.

Looking back at the house, Gracy was so worried about Elaine being there with that mean old man all alone, but she knew she could not make her come. As the rest of the children followed Gracy to her cottage each one was asking questions about why Elaine did not want to come with them. Gracy explained to them the best she could so no one would want to run back. Then she said, "We must hurry. We should try to get to my cottage before it gets dark. I have had enough of dark paths."

After everyone had gone, Elaine closed the door as tight as she could, then she went back through the house and started to do everything the others didn't get a chance to do. After about an hour, Elaine started to get extremely tired. Her body was not used to working that fast, trying to get everything done so before the old man got home. She knew she could not stop for even a moment so the old man wouldn't notice that the others were gone.

Running in fear, Emily's little legs were completely tired. Tony picked her up and said, "I will carry you the rest of the way. Are the rest of you okay?"

As the sun started to set Gracy, Tony, Emily, Lee, and Mike were almost to Gracy's cottage. Even though it had been a long time, she could tell they were almost there. Lee tripped so many times with his big shoes, but he wasn't hurt. Different things happened on the long walk. All of them were scared and happy at the same time while trying to figure out what would come next. Reaching a safe distance, they were able to slow down to an easy walk.

On the way, Gracy started telling everyone about what she saw the last few times she went to the pond. "I always felt like someone was watching me, but when I turned around, there's no one there. But one day I saw something or someone out of the corner of my eye," Gracy explained.

"Do you think it was a person?" said Tony.

"Or a thing?" said Lee as he tripped a little with his big shoes.

"I'm not sure," said Gracy. "But I would love to know what it is."

"But we can talk about that later," said Tony. "We need to hurry!"

"Yeah, it is starting to get dark," said Lee.

So everyone started walking a little faster. This time it was fun to walk fast; they laughed and told some funny stories. Lee did not say much. He was looking all around, noticing how the forest was changing the closer they got to Gracy's cottage. He saw some of the most beautiful flowers and trees. It reminded him of when his mom took care of the flowers at their house before the old man took over.

Lee touched Emily on her leg and said, "Don't this place remind you of mom?"

Emily just nodded her head and started looking around. When Mike looked at the two of them and saw the smiles on their faces, he knew they did the right thing by running away.

*****

Meanwhile, Elaine was still doing all of the work. Feeling a little faint, she sat down for a moment. All of a sudden she heard the old man unlocking the door. *Oh no, the old man is home.* Elaine had not finished everything.

"I don't smell my dinner!" he yelled.

Oh no! Elaine thought. That's the one thing she did not have a chance to do. She said, "It will be on the table soon." So Elaine started to put things on the stove fast as she could.

When the old man started to walk around the house, he only saw Elaine. He yelled, "Hey, girl, where is everyone?"

"I don't know," said Elaine in a very shaky voice.

"What do you mean you don't know?" the old man yelled even louder.

Elaine was so terrified she could not say another word.

The old man's eyebrows went up, and his eyes turned red. Then he started to run through the house. "Where are they? Where are they?" he yelled over and over again. "Where is my complete set, three girls and three boys?" The old man ran so fast around the house that Elaine dropped to her knees and begged him to stop. "You're going to tell me where they are." The old man grabbed Elaine. "Where are they?"

With tears in her eyes, she screamed, "They're out there! They went to Gracy's cottage down the path."

"Why?" the old man yelled.

"To get away from you. They all ran away from you." With her hands over her face, she continued to cry, knowing she just couldn't hold the secret any longer. she just might have gotten everyone caught.

"How did they do that? I had a spell on them."

"They stopped drinking the water, and they're getting older!" said Elaine.

"They broke my spell. They broke my spell…" The old man was furious to think a bunch of children had outsmarted him. "You're going to help me get them back," the old man said to Elaine.

*****

By this time Gracy, Tony, Mike, Emily, and Lee had made it to Gracy's small cottage. It looked so different than she remembered it, but it was pleasing to the eyes. There was Gracy's list of things she was planning to do once she was young. She just looked at it. The cottage was a little dusty and stuffy. *It's been a long time since I was here.* Right away she ran to look in the white mirror trimmed in pink that her mom had given her when she was a child the first time. Gracy was happy to see that she was getting older again. Standing beside her was Tony; he was much older as well. But Emily, Lee, and Mike were not. They told Gracy, "We were young from the start, and we're brothers and sister. Our parents passed away. The old man was our friend who came to help. The house the old man lives in now used to be ours."

"That's why I took my favorite doll," said Emily. "My mom made it for me."

"And I like my big shoes," said Lee. "They were my dad's."

"You all know about my jacket, said Mike. "My mom made it too."

Mike, Emily, and Lee continued to tell their story. "The old man used to live in the house just before you get to the pond down the dark path." Gracy remembered when she first saw that house the night she followed the old man. "When he found out that the water from the pond kept us young, that's all we were allowed to drink. Then he started to make us do everything around the house. And he treated us badly."

"Emily cries every night. I wanted to give her a hug," said Lee. "But the old man would not let me."

"One time Lee dropped some food on the floor, and the old man made him clean the whole big house by himself before he could go to bed," said Mike.

"I wonder why he wanted us," said Tony.

"He was always talking about his complete set," said Gracy. "It's all behind us now. We should not ever have to worry about the old man again."

As Gracy was talking, Tony said to her, "We are actually about the same age. The old man caught me drinking from the pond and pushed me in. When I pulled myself out, I was a child. I lived alone on the other side of the pond. The reason I lived alone was I never met the right person for me, so I never married or had children."

"Same thing happened to me," said Gracy.

Tony looked at her and said, "When you first came to the house, our lives started getting better right away. The old man changed just a little, then it's like he started to get comfortable with us, and that gave us a chance to get our lives back."

"But what if he figured out where we are and come and get us?" said Mike.

"We are bigger and older now. We can protect ourselves," said Tony.

"Will we be able to go outside and play?" said Lee.

"Not for a few days. We have to make sure the old man doesn't find us. He will definitely try to start trouble," said Gracy.

After they all had shared their stories of how they met the old man, they just sat for a few minutes with some much-needed rest. They all got up and started to clean the cottage not because they had to but because they wanted to.

Emily started in the kitchen because that's what she was used to.

"I'll take out the trash," said Mike.

Lee said, "All we have are some old fruits and berries. I have nothing to clean."

"You don't have to do anything if you don't want to," said Gracy. Then she danced through the cottage and opened all the windows just to smell the flowers, hear the birds sing, and see how the wind blew through the trees. It was so good to be home to live her life the way she always wanted.

As the family was settling in and everyone was finding their place in the home, there was a knock on the door. Lee ran to open the door, and Tony stopped him by saying, "Wait, let me open it."

So Tony eased over to the door with his back to the wall. He reached and grabbed something heavy. Then he put his hand on the doorknob, turning it slowly, and opened it fast. Just when he was ready to swing, he saw it was Elaine standing there with the blue bucket of water. Her face was red, and she was extremely dirty and sweaty. "Elaine, how did you get away?" said Tony.

Just then Gracy ran to get her with a wet cloth for her face.

"I had to finish everyone's work after you all left. I was trying to make sure the old man didn't notice that everyone was gone for a while, but he noticed right away because I forgot to cook." As Elaine was talking, everyone noticed she was also holding a baby wrapped in a homemade blanket.

"Where did you get that baby?" Mike asked.

"Yeah, where did it come from?" said Lee.

"Sure, is a funny-looking thing," said Emily.

Gracy took one look at the baby and said as she handed Elaine the wet cloth, "That's the old man, isn't it?"

"Yes," said Elaine. "This is the old man."

"Oh lord, what happened to him? Did you push him into the pond or something?" asked Tony.

She explained to them that she was her right age and she never had to drink any of the water from the pond. "I and the old man were the only ones who could drink the water from the well that was in the silver bucket. So once you figured out the secret in the water, I knew it was just a matter of time before you would be able to escape. While you were starting your plan, I was starting mine. I always saved another blue bucket of water."

"So you knew all along what I've been doing to the water," said Gracy.

"Not at first, but when I saw Emily and Lee started to look a little different, I started watching you, Gracy," said Elaine.

"But I wonder why the old man didn't notice," said Tony.

"Because he's old and can't see well, and he is blind in one eye." Then Elaine continued to tell how when the old man noticed that they were gone, he started to run around the house, looking for everyone and yelling for them. "It was so bad," said Elaine. "He made me tell him where you were. He was so angry, and I was so afraid of him that I dropped to the floor and yelled out everything."

"But how did he turn into a baby?" asked Lee.

Elaine continued to explain. "When he was running around the house, screaming to the top of his lungs, asking where was everyone, he was sweating very hard. So I ran and grabbed the blue bucket of water and dumped it on his head to cool him down. Next thing I knew, he had turned into a baby."

"An ugly baby," said Mike.

"After that I didn't know what to do, so I wrapped him in a blanket and started down the dark path to get more water from the pond, then I started to find everyone, walking back down the dark path past our old house."

"Wait, Tony said, "you said *our*."

"Yes," said Elaine. "You see, the old man took me from my mom and dad. I'm not sure where my parents are now." Elaine continued to tell her story. "I passed our old house, and I could see it had not changed a bit. He must have been going there all along keeping it up."

"Yes. The night I followed him, he stopped at that house. I always wondered why," said Gracy.

"Then I decided to look for all of you and saw this cottage and stopped. I'm so glad I found you. Now I need to know what to do with the little old man-baby."

"What if he starts to grow?" said Lee.

"So that's why you brought the bucket of water here," said Emily with a smile on her face.

Elaine said, "Yes, just in case."

Then Gracy took one look at the old man-baby and said, "I will keep him and raise him to be a good man."

"We will raise him to be a good man," said Tony. Then he got down on one knee and asked Gracy to marry him.

Gracy took one look at him with happy tears in her eyes, smiled, and said, "Yes, I will marry you, Tony."

Mike started to dance around, Emily grabbed her face with a big smile, and Lee looked and said, "Yuck!"

Elaine said, "You are going to be the old man-baby's parents?"

They started to laugh. Then Gracy jumped with happiness and excitement.

"We are going to have a wedding," said Emily.

It was very entertaining dancing to the beat of each person's own drum. Then Lee yelled out, "What about us?" Everyone stopped and looked at him. Lee said it again but in a soft voice, "What about us?"

Gracy went over to him and said, "Would you take me to be your mom to have and to hold from this day forward for the rest of my life?"

"Yes," said Lee. "But what about my brother and sister?"

Gracy looked at Emily, then Mike. "Will you take me as your mom?"

Emily and Mike said yes as well.

Everyone gathered around Lee and hugged one another. In the middle of it all, the old man-baby started to cry. "What is wrong with him?" said Emily.

"He's probably hungry," said Gracy.

"We have fruits and berries!" said Lee, smiling.

Then Gracy handed the old man-baby to Elaine. "Hold him while I go and mash him up something," said Gracy.

After they all calmed down and the old man-baby had been fed, Gracy said, "Let's all settle in for the night. We will figure out everything in the morning. We have a big day ahead of us."

*****

Once everyone had eaten, taken bath, and found their place to sleep, Tony decided to walk and see if his house was still standing. It had been years. Even though it was dark, he wasn't afraid. When Tony arrived at his house, it was not what he had expected. Someone was living in it. He took one look through the window. It was a family—a husband, a wife, and two children. Tony smiled and said to himself, "They can have it. I have a new life and family now." Then he went to spend the night at the house they all lived with the old man. Now that the old man was a baby and Tony was older, he was not worried about anything.

*****

The next morning Gracy woke up early, opened all the windows, and said to everyone, "Let's eat breakfast, and then we will all go and take another look at the other two houses." Putting on the same clothes from the day before they all started to walk there.

"But where is Tony?" said Lee.

"I'm sure he's okay," said Gracy.

Then Mike and Lee went out to gather food for breakfast. There were all kinds of fruits and berries. They picked as much as they needed and nothing more. There were fresh eggs and sugarcane, honey, and all kinds of fresh things.

When Tony returned to the cottage, he had meat, and Gracy was feeding the old man-baby. By this time the boys had returned with everything they had as well. Gracy and the girls made hot bread with honey and something sweet to drink with no water added.

As they sat at the table to eat, everyone was very quiet. Finally Mike said, "We don't have to be quiet anymore, do we, Gracy?"

Emily said, "Ouch! My bread is hot." She put her finger in her mouth to cool off the slight burn."

"But it's good," said Lee. "And you didn't have to clean it." Then everyone got quiet as if they had done something wrong.

"No, we do not have to be quiet anymore. You can all talk as much as you want."

There was not a word from anyone. All of a sudden Tony started to laugh. "Now that we can talk, no one has anything to say." Then they all started to laugh and talk at the same time. It was the best breakfast ever until that old man-baby started to cry.

"What is wrong with him now?" said Emily.

"I don't know," said Gracy.

"He's not wet or hungry. Is he sick?" said Tony.

"Not sure," said Gracy.

"I think he's just mad that he's a baby," said Emily.

"Yeah, that's it," Emily and Mike said together.

After breakfast, just as they had planned, Gracy, Tony, Elaine, Lee, Emily, and Mike all walked back past the house where they lived together with the old man. Down the path to the other house, Gracy remembered passing every time she went to get the water from the pond. Once they got there, everyone seemed to be too afraid to go in. Finally Tony said, "I will go in first." So he walked up to the door and turned the knob. It was open! He opened his eyes wide so he could see as he walked into the dark and cold room. After his eyes adjusted to the dim light in the house, Tony began to check every room and everything.

While standing on the outside, Gracy and the rest of the children were in position to either run or wait for Tony to say come in. After he checked half-way through the house, Gracy said to the children, "I think it's okay to go in. Follow me."

Mike, Emily, and Lee held onto her and then to one another. They walked in. Elaine was the last one to enter the house because she was carrying the old man-baby because they knew he wouldn't cry if she was the one holding him. Everyone was in, but Tony was still searching through the house, making sure every part was safe. When he saw that everyone was in, he instructed them to stay up front.

"Okay, let your eyes adjust to the light," said Gracy. Then right away she opened all the curtains and slid open all the windows in the room. "Now we can all see better. Did you check down the hall, Tony?"

"No," said Tony.

As he started walking down a long hall toward the back of the house, Emily held onto the back of her brother Mike's shirt. "You are choking me," said Mike.

Emily let go of his shirt and grabbed his hand. "Is that better?" she said.

Mike just looked at her and smiled.

As they walked together with his big shoes making clonking sounds on the floor, Lee looked at them both and made the shushing sound with one finger up to his mouth and a frown on his face. "I think he's scared," Emily said to Mike. Then they both let out a little laugh.

By this time Tony had reached the back of the house. He entered what was the kitchen. As he walked through the door coming around the corner, he came face-to-face with a woman with long red matted hair with a flower tucked behind her right ear along with a few strings of hair. She was very pale and thin and looked like an older version of Elaine. Tony jumped when she screamed, "Who are you?"

"Who, me?" said Tony.

"Yes, you," said the woman.

When the others heard the scream, they ran down the long hall. Elaine was last in the back, still holding the old man-baby, trying to see who Tony was talking to.

"I'm Nancy," said the woman.

Elaine could hear the woman's voice. She could not believe her ears. She pushed through so she could get a better look. When she saw the redheaded woman, she started crying. In a soft but trembling voice, she said, "Mom?"

Nancy said, "Elaine, is that you?"

"Oh yes, Mom, it is me." Elaine gave the baby to Gracy and took two big steps, and she was in her mother's arms.

Elaine embraced her mom, who said, "Oh, E, I've missed you so much. Ever since we lost you at the pond, we have never stopped looking."

"How did you get separated?" said Gracy.

"One day we were at the pond down the path, sitting and having family time. Elaine went to gather rocks and flowers on the other side, and this strange old man came out of nowhere and said that the pond belonged to him and we needed to leave. Of course we didn't go right away. I was packing up our things so we wouldn't leave anything, but I guess we took too long. When we looked for Elaine, she was gone. We looked everywhere for her. I would take a walk to the pond every day and sit for hours just in case she came back.

"One day the old man was there. I asked him if he had, and he said, 'I don't know an Elaine, but I'm going to have my complete set one day.' Then he dipped his bucket in the water and walked off. I would see him at least once a week. One night he stopped here and said I needed to stop going to his pond if I knew what was best for me. Most of the time I would see him on his way to the pond. Then one day he stopped coming around. One day I decided to go to the pond to look for my daughter, and I saw a little blonde-haired girl walking down the path with the bucket. I wanted to say something to her, but I was afraid I would scare her or worse, so I watched from afar."

"That was me," said Gracy. "The old man trusted me to get the water from the pond."

While Gracy was talking, Nancy kissed Elaine on her forehead, squeezed her tight, and said, "I never want to let you go, but I wondered why and where he took you. And how did you get away from that mean old man? And who are your friends."

Elaine started to explain. "He grabbed me when you were taking a drink from the pond. He dipped his bucket in the water and rushed me to this big beautiful house down the path. We all were his slaves. Not sure why he wanted us there."

"I think he was lonely and just wanted a family," said Gracy.

"Yes, he was holding us as slaves," said Tony.

"But why are you in the old man's house?" said Lee.

"This is our house," said Elaine.

"His house is the little old house sitting by the ditch," said Gracy.

"We hardly ever went to town or the market or anything. We stayed here to be close to the pond so we could find you, Elaine," said Nancy.

"We who?" said Emily.

Nancy took one look at Elaine and said, "Your father is out back." She looked toward the back door and started making her way across the kitchen floor, looking down at her mother's dirty feet and the black diamond pattern on the tile. She walked out the back door. At the same time, Nancy looked at Tony and Gracy and asked how they got away. They all took turns telling her the story about the water, the pond, the well water, the whole plan, and how each of them was caught by the old man. Then Nancy looked at Gracy holding the baby. "So this is the old man?" said Nancy.

"Yes. Thanks to your daughter, we don't have to worry about him ever again," said Gracy.

While everyone was talking about their time in the house with the old man, Elaine walked out the back door. There she saw her dad working in the garden. She saw all kinds of vegetables; some were the ones the old man would bring to the big house for them to eat. She looked at the grass that needed to be badly cut. But it didn't really matter. She looked at her father with his white-and-black hair. His sunburned face was already starting to peal, and his clothes badly needed to be washed. With all of that, her father was the most handsome man she'd ever seen.

Elaine stood and watched him for a second. She was so thankful and glad to see him. With tears streaming down her face, Elaine called out to her father, "Pop!"

Her father turned around. He could not believe his eyes. "Elaine, my darling daughter?" he said.

"Yes, Poppa, it's me," she said.

Her father dropped the garden tool he had in his hand, pulled off his gloves, and ran out of the garden across the field so he could hug his beautiful redheaded daughter. "How did you get away from that old man,?"

Elaine told her father the story, then she said, "Come and meet my friends, Poppa."

So they walked back upstairs, and her father removed his hat before he walked through the back door into the house where everyone was still standing in the kitchen. Elaine pointed over to the right of the kitchen and said, "This is Gracy. She was the last person the old man had brought to the house."

"Yes, he pushed me into the pond, and I became a little girl again," said Gracy.

"And this is Tony." She pointed to him.

"He did the same to me," said Tony.

"And these three are siblings Mike, Lee, and Emily. Their mother and father died, and the old man was a friend of the family who came to help, but he took over their house and turned them into his slaves instead. And this baby is the old man."

Her father looked at the baby in disbelief. "What!" he said.

"Yes," said Elaine. "I dumped the pond water on his head, and he turned into a baby. I will tell you the complete story after we all figure out what we are going to do."

"So what should we do now?" Elaine's father said.

"Anything we want to do," said Tony.

"I would love for us all to stay close together," said Gracy. Tony and I are going to get married and take care of Mike, Lee, Emily, and the old man-baby. If you like, Nancy, you three can move into my cottage. Since the big house belongs to the children anyway, we could turn it back into a loving home."

"That won't be necessary," said Nancy. "We will just stay here. Now that the old man is gone and we have our daughter back, life will be better than ever."

"Okay." Gracy looked at Tony. "I think we should be getting back. We have a lot to do."

Then Elaine reached out and hugged Gracy, Tony, Mike, Lee, and Emily and said, "I will come and visit as often as I can, and you all are welcome to come here anytime. Thank you so much for helping me find my parents."

They said their goodbyes and their see-you-laters and headed back toward the big house. The closer they got to the house, the harder Gracy's heart started to beat. Tony took her by the hand and said, "It's going to be okay." This time, when they all approached the house, it was with joy, not fear. Gracy stopped to take a look at the well as she and her new family walked by and up to the brown door of the big beautiful house. She turned the knob and pushed the door open and walked in. Tony, Mike, Lee, and Emily followed.

"What should we do first?" said Emily.

"Anything you like," said Gracy as she looked around to see where to start herself. It all looked the same, only she could tell that the old man had run around, turning things over looking for them. She glanced down at the baby boy in her arms and said, "You made quite a mess, didn't you?" For some reason, by the smile on his face, she knew he understood her, and she could feel he had gotten a little heavier.

"Okay, let's get to work," said Tony.

"Right away," Mike said with the biggest smile on his face. "I will take out the trash."

"I will clean the kitchen," said Emily.

"Before you get started, Emily," said Gracy, "I have something for you." She pulled out a pair of long white socks for her to wear so she wouldn't scrape her legs on the ladder anymore.

"Oh, thank you!" said Emily.

Lee asked if they could have a snack before they got started. Gracy went over to the pantry, pulled out the best they had to eat, and gave it to him. After he finished, he was ready to work. Gracy pulled down all the worn and torn curtains and opened the windows just to hear the birds sing, smell the flowers, and see the wind blowing through the trees. It all needed to be done. The rugs were pulled up to be dusted, the floors were cleaned, and the walls were washed down. The five of them worked up into the night. The house never looked better. The children's rooms were put back together to match their personalities. It was the greatest feeling they felt in a long time.

As all this cleaning was going on, the old man-baby started to cry. "I guess he is hungry," said Tony.

So Gracy stopped what she was doing to feed the baby. Then it hit her. *I have a family, I am a mom, and I'm getting married.* After she finished feeding the baby, she put him down for a nap and said to everyone, "I will be right back." Gracy took off down the path to her cottage. She ran straight through the door to her room and grabbed the big white mirror trimmed in pink that her mother gave her when she was a child and ran back with it. Now that she was young, Gracy can really run. She returned to the house with her mirror and went to her new room and secured it to the wall. Gracy took one look at herself. There were no wrinkles on her face. She was a young woman and not a child. *Tomorrow we will go back to my cottage to get the rest of our things. We will get everything we need to make this big house a home.* Gracy took another look at herself in the mirror. Her old dress and shoes were beginning to fit again but better.

"That's a nice big mirror," said Tony.

"Thank you," said Gracy. "My mom gave it to me when I was a child, and I have loved it ever since."

"Is it okay if I look at myself sometimes?" said Emily.

"Of course you can anytime you like," said Gracy. "Tomorrow when will go back to my cottage, we will pack up everything we need to make this house feel like home."

After a good night's rest, the next morning Gracy decided to get up early and go to the cottage before everyone else. She needed time to walk alone and reflect on everything that had happened. She was at the cottage in no time. She walked into the house and straight to her room and started to pull everything out of her closet. She started to look for something to pack her things in. As she pulled the last thing out of the closet, Gracy saw a wooden box on the right side, at the bottom of it. She got on her knees and pulled the box into the middle of her bedroom floor and tried to open it. *I'm going to need something to help me break this lock.* So she went into the other room and found a hammer. With it in her hand, Gracy sat back on the floor and hit the lock upward. It worked! After putting the hammer down, she pulled the box closer to her. Gracy picked what was inside—it was a beautiful wedding gown. *It must have been my mother's,* she thought. Right away Gracy pulled it out, checked for rips and holes, and made sure it was clean. Everything was fine. *It is so beautiful,* she thought. She pulled it close to her body, and she just had to try it on. It was a perfect fit.

Standing in the wedding dress and looking down at it all the way to the hem, she whispered, "It is the most beautiful dress I have ever seen. Thank you, Mommy." There were pearls all over it, satin flowers trimmed around the neck and down the sleeves, and a bow on each shoulder and one on the back. There was also a matching coat with an extra set of satin and pearls on the neckline and a matching dress with satin flowers as well. At the bottom of the wooden box, there were a pair of satin white shoes that went perfectly with the dress. Gracy could not do another thing. She just wanted to dance around in her dress. As she was spinning, she felt a sharp pain in her back. "Oh no," she said. Looking at her hands, Gracy could see some wrinkles. *I don't need to start hurting for my wedding,* Gracy thought. *I will just drink a little bit of the pond water to get me through it.* So she walked to her kitchen, got the bucket, made herself a small glass of water, and took one sip. The wrinkles started to disappear. One more sip, and her back pain was gone.

Still standing in the wedding dress, she could hear the rest of her family coming. So she hurried and put her wedding dress away, drank the rest of the water, and waited for everyone to come in. Then one by one everyone came in. Gracy said, "Let's eat breakfast before we get started." After they all had eaten, they each grabbed something and walked back to the big house. After three trips, they thought the move was complete. But Gracy said, "One more trip, and I just need Tony." She wanted him to help her with the wooden box. "Mike, Lee, and Emily can start putting everything away. When we get back, I will cook dinner after feeding the old man-baby and putting him to sleep."

Gracy and Tony walked to the cottage one last time. Gracy was so excited to go back to get the wooden box. When they returned with it, everyone wanted to know what was in it. "I will let everyone know in a few days. Until then you'll just have to wait," Gracy said.

Now Gracy was happy to make dinner for her new family, Emily started helping Lee to set the table. While he was clonking around in his big old shoes, he tripped and fell. "Are you okay?" asked Tony.

Lee, still sitting on the floor, just nodded his head up and down, saying yes.

"Tomorrow we will try to find you some new shoes that will fit until you grow into the ones you have on right now."

The next day they all got up early, ate breakfast, and set out to the market. "We have to find Lee some new shoes and get things for the wedding," said Gracy. They didn't have any money, but Tony had a gold pocket watch that he was willing to trade. "Are you sure you want to give up your father's watch?"

Tony said, "Gracy, my dad would have done the same thing. Now let's go and have some fun."

The first place they stopped was the trade store. Tony walked in first and started talking to the owner of the store. "Hello, I would like to trade this gold pocket watch for cash please," said Tony.

"Let me take a look at it," said the owner. "Oh yes, this is a fine watch you have here. How much did you want for it?"

"How much do you think it is worth?" said Tony.

"Okay, I will let you have whatever you need out of my store for the watch," said the store owner.

"That's a deal," said Tony.

So Lee picked out new black shoes, two shirts, and two pairs of pants. Emily got five new dresses and shoes. Mike got shirts, shoes, new pants, and a hat. Gracy got everything she needed for her wedding—cake and food. "What are you getting for yourself, Tony?" said Gracy.

"I don't want or need anything," said Tony.

"Yes, you do," said Gracy. "Get a new suit for our wedding."

Just when Tony was going to say yes, the old man-baby started to cry.

"We know what that means," said Mike.

"Yes, said Emily.

"He's hungry," said Lee.

Just when Gracy was getting ready to feed the baby, he knocked the bottle out of her hand.

"What is wrong with him?" said Tony.

"He probably thinks it's water. Oh," said Emily.

"Right now we will give him some real food," said Gracy.

Now the shopping trip was over, and everyone was tired and ready to go home. Tony made sure everyone was safe in the house before he went to Gracy's cottage. "I will see everyone tomorrow," said Tony.

*****

Now when Gracy walked into the house, her pain was back, but she didn't have any water there. That was the one thing she forgot. *Oh well, I'll get some in the morning.* So the next morning Gracy could hardly get out of bed. *I have to get that water. I am getting old too fast.* As she walked across the room to check on the baby, he was gone. Gracy started to panic. *Where is that little old man-baby?* She walked all over the house. When she found him, he was walking and was trying to reach the lock on the door. When he saw Gracy, he started to run. With her getting older, he was moving too fast. Gracy called for Mike,

Emily, and Lee to help her catch him. The children came running.

"It is the old man-baby!" said Lee.

"When did he start walking?" said Mike.

Emily just sat down, watched, and laughed. It was the funniest thing to see—everyone trying to catch the old man-baby. Then Emily looked at Gracy. "Gracy, you are old!" she said.

Gracy stopped chasing the old man-baby and went to look in the mirror. By the time she had reached her room, Mike had caught the baby. Lee yelled out, "Mike got him, Gracy." But she didn't hear him. She was standing in her room, looking at old Gracy again. *I don't think Tony will want to marry me now that I'm an old woman.* She pulled her hands through her white hair as if it were a comb. Gracy looked at the wrinkles on her face and hands. *Well, I'm old Gracy again.* When she turned around, all three children, with Mike still holding the baby, were looking at her with big smiles on their faces.

"Momma, you are beautiful," said Emily. Then they all came to hug her.

"Okay, let me get myself together, and I will fix breakfast." So Gracy took the old man-baby from Mike and said, "I will be out in a few minutes. Now you, little man, if you want me to let you grow up, you better behave yourself." After Gracy got herself dressed, she went out to the kitchen to cook for her family.

"When is Tony coming over?" said Lee.

"I am not sure," said Gracy. Deep down inside Gracy was nervous about Tony seeing her. Then there was a knock on the door.

Mike jumped up and said, "That has to be him."

Gracy braced herself because she was a little worried.

"It is Elaine, said Emily.

They all ran to give her a hug. "We missed you," said Lee.

"Yes," said Emily.

Mike just smiled and said, "Look at the old man-baby. He is walking and trying to run away."

"He has grown so much," said Elaine. "Do you still have the bucket of water I gave you?"

"It is at my cottage with Tony. I hope he remembers to bring it."

While they were all talking about the baby, Elaine was looking at Gracy, thinking to herself that she was a beautiful old lady. Then Lee and Mike asked if they could go outside. When the two boys opened the door, there was Tony. "Where are you two going?" he asked.

"Just outside," said Lee.

Tony walked into the house and saw Gracy. He was in love all over again, for he was an old man as well.

Then Elaine said, "I need to tell you both something. The pond is drying up. We have not had any rain. We need to get the blue bucket from the cottage to make sure the old man-baby grows slowly. If he grows too fast, there is no telling what he might do."

"Do not worry," said Tony. "I will get it. That little old man needs to stay little."

"Okay. Now, Gracy," said Elaine, "we need to get ready for your wedding."

"Yes, thank you. I will need a lot of help. Nothing fancy. Short and sweet. Now that Tony is gone, I can pull out my dress. I need help pulling the box out."

So Gracy and Elaine pulled the wooden box out together. When Gracy opened it, she got the same feeling she had when she opened it for the first time.

"Oh, it is beautiful!" said Elaine. "Absolutely beautiful!"

"And there is a coat and shoes to match," said Gracy. "Now that I am older, I think I need to try it on again." Gracy pulled the dress up to her, then slipped it on. It was still a perfect fit; the shoes and the coat all fit. "Tomorrow I will be married. All my dreams are coming true." Then Gracy took off the coat, the shoes, and the dress. She put them back in the box, sat down on the bed, and looked off into space.

"What are you thinking about?" said Elaine.

"Just thinking how I wanted to be young so bad that I was willing to go to great lengths for it. In the process, I became a slave."

"But if you had not come to the house, we will all still be there, and the old man would still have us," said Elaine. "It was bad, but you were our miracle and angel."

Then Gracy told Elaine about the image she saw when she went to the pond when they were living with the old man, "I am still wondering what that was."

Then Emily ran into the room. The old man-baby was running around and throwing things all over the house. By the time Gracy and Elaine got there, he was sitting down like a good little boy. "Okay, little man, let's get you ready for bed. We can all eat dinner and start getting ready for tomorrow."

That night, after everyone had eaten and had their baths, they all decide to sit and tell funny stories that they could not talk about when they were living with the old man. They laughed and talked into the night.

*****

The day of the wedding was finally here. Everyone was doing everything they could to help. The yard was fixed with flowers and all kinds of trimmings. So much delicious food to eat—that was Lee's favorite part, and he was ready for it all. Emily decided to put on one of her dresses that Tony got with his gold pocket watch; it was pink to match her doll's. Elaine's parents arrived and noticed the old man-baby was bigger and was walking around. "I think the old man-baby is growing too fast," said Nancy.

"Yes," said Elaine's dad. Then they both went to find a seat for the wedding.

Gracy was in her room, getting ready. It was the most wonderful day ever. *I am getting married,* she thought as she looked at herself in the big white mirror trimmed in pink that her mother gave her when she was a child. *And Tony loves just the way I am, old woman and all.* With her new friends and family, Gracy was ready to live her new life. Then she remembered. *We do not have a preacher.* She called for Elaine. "We do not have a preacher. What am I going to do?" said Gracy.

"You do not have to worry, Gracy," said Elaine. "My father is a preacher. His name is George. I will let him know."

Now with George and everyone in place, the wedding could start. Gracy was in her all-white gown with pearls, satin flowers, bows, and perfectly matched coat and shoes. She walked out of the house past everyone down to Tony. Gracy was thinking how handsome Tony was, and he was smiling and thinking how beautiful she was.

As Gracy reached the front, Tony took her hand, and George started the ceremony. Gracy and Tony decided to speak from their hearts. Elaine and Nancy started to cry happy tears. As soon as George said "I pronounce you man and wife," the old man-baby started to scream. He jumped off his seat and started to run around, kicking up dirt around Gracy. Finally Elaine grabbed him and took the little old man-baby into the house. Then Gracy and Tony were married.

"You may kiss the bride."

Emily smiled and tossed up some flowers.

Mike went and shook Tony's hand and said, "Congratulations!"

Lee said, "Yuck!"

Elaine kept the old man-baby in the house until everything was over.

Gracy came inside to check on Elaine and the baby. She had gone to sleep, and the old man-baby was gone. Everyone looked all over for him but could not find him. "Maybe he went out the back door we used to escape," said Tony. So they all went to the back door, and there was the old man-baby lying on the floor, fast asleep.

"I guess he was too short or weak to push it open."

Gracy asked Tony if he had brought the water in the blue bucket. He said yes. Then she went to get a bath cloth, dipped it in the water, and washed the old man-baby with it. "We will make sure he grows slowly and teach him to be a good man."

Then Gracy said, "I now have the family I always wanted and a life of happiness." She picked up the baby, looked down at him, and smiled. He smiled back.

The next morning Gracy got up early with her new family and opened the windows so they could smell the flowers, listen to the birds sing, and see how the wind blew through the trees. "We will never have to go to the pond again. I will never have to worry about whatever that was I saw."

"I think it was a bird," said Tony. "The last time I was there, this bird dropped down in front of me."

"So all this time I was afraid of a bird?"

They all laughed, and they lived happily ever after, or did they?

About the Author

Antoinette Sidberry Richardson currently lives in New Bern, NC where she was raised. She is a loving mother, wife, and first-time author. She started as a professional model with the Ruth Anne Modeling Agency. She later began writing *The Secret in the Water* about six years prior after having her daughter and gaining inspiration from her. Richardson is excited to share her writings with you and the world.